The Princess and the Raven

and other princess stories

Compiled by Tig Thomas

Miles
KeLLy

First published in 2013 by Miles Kelly Publishing Ltd
Harding's Barn, Bardfield End Green, Thaxted, Essex, CM6 3PX, UK

Copyright © Miles Kelly Publishing Ltd 2013

2 4 6 8 10 9 7 5 3 1

Publishing Director Belinda Gallagher
Creative Director Jo Cowan
Editorial Director Rosie McGuire
Senior Editor Claire Philip
Senior Designer Joe Jones
Production Manager Elizabeth Collins
Reprographics Stephan Davis, Jennifer Hunt, Thom Allaway

ISBN 978-1-78209-213-1

Printed in China

British Library Cataloguing-in-Publication Data
A catalogue record for this book is available from the British Library

ACKNOWLEDGEMENTS

The publishers would like to thank the following artists who have contributed to this book:
Smiljana Coh, Marcin Piwowarski, Mélanie Florian, Kirsten Wilson, Jacqueline East (cover)

All other artwork from the Miles Kelly Artwork Bank

The publishers would like to thank the following sources for the use of their photographs:
Cover frame: Karina Bakalyan/Shutterstock.com
Inside frame: asmjp/Shutterstock.com

Made with paper from a sustainable forest
www.mileskelly.net   info@mileskelly.net

Contents

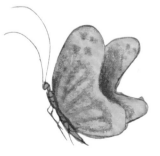

The Unseen Bridegroom

By Joseph Jacobs

ONCE UPON A TIME there was a king and queen with three beautiful daughters. The most beautiful was the youngest, and her name was Anima.

One day all three sisters were playing in the meadows, and Anima saw a bush with lovely flowers. As she pulled it up to plant in her own garden she plucked at the root, which gave way. Anima saw beneath it a stairway going down into the earth. Being a brave girl, she crept down the stairs for

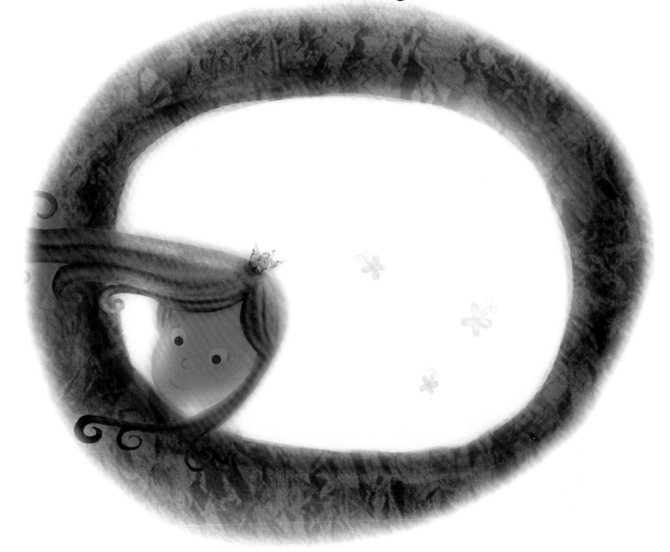

a long, long way, until at last she came out into the open air. Not far away, in front of her, she saw a magnificent palace.

Anima ran towards it, and when she came to the gates, they opened without anybody being there. Anima went in and found it marvellously decorated. She came to a room with cosy couches, and sat down.

Immediately a table appeared before her, with fruits and cakes and cool drinks upon it. So Anima took as much as she needed, fell asleep and did not awake until it was getting dark. She cried out, "Oh, I must go back to my father and mother, how shall I go? How shall I go?"

Then the voice of a young man spoke out saying, "Stay with me and be my bride, and you shall have all your heart desires."

But Anima cried out, "Let me see you!"

The voice replied, "That is forbidden. You must never look on my face, for my mother, the queen, has forbidden me to marry and laid a spell on me."

So sweet and gentle was his voice that Anima agreed to marry him, and they lived happily together, though he never came near her till all was dark, so that she could not see him. But after a time Anima became curious as to what manner of man her husband might be.

The next night Anima lit a candle and looked at her husband while he was sleeping. She was delighted to discover a most handsome man.

But then three drops of wax fell upon his cheek and woke him up. He knew she had broken her promise.

"Oh, Anima," he said, "why have you done this? We must part until you can persuade my mother to break the spell."

With that came a rumbling of thunder and the flame of Anima's candle went out, the palace disappeared and she found herself on a bleak moor.

She walked till she came to a house where an old woman greeted her. Anima explained what had happened, and the old woman said, "I see. You have married my sister's son, and I fear she will never forgive you. If you go to her and ask for your husband, she'll give him up to you if you do everything that she asks. Take this twig. If she asks what I think she will, strike it on the ground three times and help will come."

So Anima set out to find the queen. After a while she came to the palace of the queen — the mother of her invisible husband — and when she came into her presence she demanded to see him.

"What!" cried the queen, "how dare you marry my son!"

"It was his choice," said Anima, "and I am now his wife. Surely you will let me see him again."

"Well," said the queen, "First you must go into a barn where my stewards have poured together wheat, oats and rice into one great heap. If by nightfall you can separate them perhaps, I may grant your request."

So Anima was led to the queen's great barn and left alone. Then she thought of the twig that the queen's sister had given her, and she struck it upon the ground.

Immediately, thousands of ants appeared and began to separate the heap of grain, taking the wheat to one corner, the oats to another, and the grains of rice to a third. By nightfall all the grain had been separated,

and when the queen came
to let Anima out she found the task had
been completed.

"You had help!" she cried. "We'll see
tomorrow if you can do something all
by yourself."

The next day the queen summoned
Anima, gave her a letter and said, "Take
this to the Queen of the Underworld,
bring back what she will give you, and
then I may let you see my son."

"How can I find her?" asked Anima.

"That you must find for yourself," the
queen said, and left her.

Poor Anima did not know which
way to go, but as she walked along the

voice of someone invisible to her said softly, "Nearby, between two steep hills, is a deep valley. Go down the valley until you come to a deep river, and there you will see an old man ferrying people across the river. Put a coin between your teeth and let him take it from you, and he will carry you across, but speak not to him. Then, on the other side, you will come to a dark cave, and at the entrance is a savage dog. Give it a loaf of bread and it will let you pass. You will soon come to the Queen of the Underworld. Take what she gives you, but beware — do not eat or drink anything while you are there."

Anima recognized the voice of her husband and did all that he had told her. When she came before the Queen of the Underworld, the queen read the letter. Then she offered Anima cake and wine, but

Amina refused, shaking her head, saying nothing. Then the Queen of the Underworld gave her a box and said she could leave.

Anima went back past the great dog and crossed the dark river. When she reached the castle again, she presented the box to the queen, who opened it and took out a wedding ring. Frowning, she said, "Someone has helped you but I cannot break my word. I suppose you must have my son."

As soon as she had said this Anima's husband appeared and took her into his arms, and they lived happily ever after.

Maid Maleen

By the Brothers Grimm

THERE WAS ONCE A PRINCESS called Maid Maleen, who was very beautiful. She fell in love with a handsome prince but her father wished her to marry another man, so her prince was sent away. However, Maid Maleen said to her father, "I will marry no other man but him, no matter what you say."

The king hated when people refused him, so he flew into a fury, and ordered a dark tower to be built, into which no ray of sunlight should enter. When it was finished, he said to his daughter, "Here you shall be imprisoned for seven years, and then I will come and see if you will agree."

Food and drink for the seven years was carried into the tower, and then Maid Maleen was led into it and walled up, and cut off from the outside world.

There she sat in the darkness, and knew not when day or night began. The time passed, and when the supply of food and drink grew small she knew that the seven years were coming to an end.

She thought someone

Maid Maleen

would come to let her out but no stroke of the hammer was heard, no stone fell out of the wall, and it seemed to Maid Maleen that her father had forgotten her.

In the end, she took a bread-knife, and picked at the mortar of a stone. She succeeded in getting out one stone, and then a second, and then a third, and when three days were over the first ray of light fell on her darkness.

At last the opening was large enough for her to see out. The sky was blue, and a fresh breeze blew, but her father's castle and all the buildings nearby lay in tumbled down ruins.

The town and the villages were, so far as could be seen, destroyed by fire, and no human being was visible. An enemy had destroyed the whole kingdom and driven away the king and all the inhabitants.

Maid Maleen climbed out of the opening and set out to find somewhere to live. After a long journey, she came to another country and went to the royal palace. At first she was ordered to go away, but at last the cook took pity on her, and said that she could have a job as a scullery maid.

The son of the king in whose kingdom she had arrived, was, however, the very man who had been betrothed to Maid Maleen all those years ago! His father had chosen another bride for him, whose face was as ugly as her heart was wicked.

The wedding date was fixed, and the ugly maiden had already arrived, but she had shut herself in her room, and allowed no one to see her. Maid Maleen had to take her meals from the kitchen.

When the day came for the bride and the bridegroom to go to church, she was ashamed of her ugliness, and afraid that if she showed herself in the streets, she would be laughed at by the people.

So she said to Maid Maleen, "I have sprained my foot, and cannot walk well. Put on my wedding clothes and take my place, just for today!"

Maid Maleen, however, refused. At last the bride said angrily, "If you do not obey me, I will order you to be killed at once."

Maid Maleen was forced to obey, and so

she put on the bride's magnificent clothes and all her jewels. When she entered the hall, everyone was amazed at her great beauty. The groom thought sadly, 'She is just like my beautiful Maid Maleen, but she has long been shut up in the tower, and may well have died.'

Then he took out a precious necklace, put it round her neck, and fastened the clasp.

They travelled to the church, and the priest married them.

Afterwards, the prince led her home to the

palace, but she did not speak a single word the whole way.

When they got back, Maid Maleen hurried into the bride's chamber, took off the magnificent wedding dress and the jewels and dressed herself in her servant's clothes. She kept on the precious necklace, which she had received from the bridegroom.

When the evening came, and the betrothed bride was led into the prince's apartment, she let her veil fall down over her face, so that he might not notice her ugly appearance.

The prince told her he liked her clothes and veil and said, "But where is the necklace I gave you at the church door?"

"What jewel?" she answered, "You gave me no jewel."

"I myself put it around your neck. If you don't know that, then you are not my true bride." He drew the veil from her face, and sprang back in surprise, and said, "Why, who are you?"

"I am your betrothed bride. But it was not me at the church — I feared the people would mock me when they saw me, so I commanded the scullery maid to dress herself in my clothes, and to go to church instead of me."

"Where is this girl?" said the prince, "Go and bring her here at once."

But instead of fetching the girl, she went out and told the servants that they must take the scullery maid into the courtyard and cut off her head.

The servants took hold of Maid Maleen but she screamed so loudly for help, that the king's son heard her voice, and ordered them to set her free. Lights were brought, and then the prince saw on her neck the necklace that he had given her at the church door.

"You are the true bride, said he, "who went with me to the church?"

She answered happily, "I am Maid Maleen, who for your sake was imprisoned for seven years in the darkness. Today, the sun is shining on me once more. I was married to you in the church, and so I am your lawful wife."

Then they kissed each other, and were

happy for the rest of their lives. The betrothed bride was banished from the kingdom as punishment for her lies.

Kate Crackernuts

A traditional Scottish fairy tale

A henwife is an old word for
a wise woman or witch.

ONCE UPON A TIME there was a king and a queen. The king had a daughter named Anne, and the queen had a daughter named Kate. Anne was far prettier than Kate, but they loved one another like real sisters. The queen was jealous that the king's daughter was prettier than her own, so she decided to try and spoil her beauty. She took advice from the henwife, who told her to send the lassie to her the next morning before she ate anything for breakfast.

Early next morning, the queen said to Anne, "Go, my dear, to the henwife in the glen, and ask her for some eggs."

Anne set out, but as she passed through the kitchen she saw a crust, and ate it.

When she came to the henwife she asked for some eggs, as she had been told to do. The henwife had laid a spell on her pot, and so she said to Anne, "Lift the lid off that pot there and see."

The lassie did so, but nothing happened.

"Go home to your mammie and tell her to keep her larder locked," said the henwife.

So she went home to the queen and told her what the henwife had said. The queen knew from this that the lassie had eaten something before she went to see the henwife, so she watched her the next morning and sent her away with nothing at all to eat.

The princess saw some country-folk picking peas by the roadside, however, and being very kind she spoke to them. They gave her a handful of the peas, which she ate as she walked.

When she came to the henwife, she was told once more, "Lift the lid off the pot and you'll see."

So Anne lifted the lid but nothing happened. The henwife angrily said to Anne, "Tell your mammie the pot won't boil if the fire's away."

So Anne went home and told the queen what she had said.

On the third day the queen went along

with the girl to the henwife. This time, however, when Anne lifted the lid off the pot, off fell her own pretty head, and on jumped a sheep's head.

So the queen was now quite satisfied. When they got back to the palace, however, Kate felt so sorry for her sister and she wanted to help her. She took a fine linen cloth and wrapped it around Anne. She took her by the hand and they both went out into the world to seek their fortune.

They went on, and on, and on, until they came to a castle. Kate knocked at the door and asked for a night's lodging for her sick sister and herself. They went in and found it was a king's castle. The king had two sons. One was very sick and no one could find out what was wrong. The curious thing was that whoever watched him at night was never seen again. So the king had offered a sack of silver to anyone who would sit up with him. Now Kate was a very brave girl, so she offered to try and help.

Up until midnight all went well. As twelve o'clock rung, however, the sick prince rose, dressed himself, and slipped downstairs. Kate followed, but he didn't seem to notice her. The prince went to the stable and saddled his horse. He called his hound then jumped into the saddle – and Kate leapt lightly up behind him.

Away rode the prince and Kate through the green wood. Kate, as they rode, plucked nuts from the trees and filled her apron with them. They rode on and on until they came to a hill. The prince stopped the horse and spoke, "Open, green hill, and let the young prince in with his horse and his hound," and Kate added, "and his lady him behind."

Immediately an opening appeared in the green hill, and they went in.

The prince entered a magnificent hall,

brightly lit.
Then many beautiful
fairies surrounded the
prince and led him off
to dance. Meanwhile
Kate, without being
noticed, hid herself behind
the door. There she saw the
prince dancing and dancing
and dancing.

At last the cockerel
crowed, and the prince made
haste to get on horseback. Kate
jumped up behind and home they
safely rode. The next
morning Kate's family

found her sitting by the fire and cracking the nuts that she had gathered the night before.

The second night passed as the first had done. The prince got up at midnight and rode away to the green hill and the fairy ball, and Kate went with him. This time she did not watch the prince, for she knew he would be dancing. She saw a fairy baby playing with a wand, and overheard one of the fairies say,

"Three strokes of that wand would make Kate's sick sister as bonnie as ever she was."

So Kate rolled nuts to the fairy baby, who

toddled after them, letting the wand fall. Then Kate took up the wand and put it in her apron.

When the cockerel crowed they rode home as before, and the moment Kate got to her room she rushed to find Anne. She tapped her with the wand three times, and the nasty sheep's head fell off and she was her own pretty self again. On the third night Kate agreed to watch again, but only if she could marry the sick prince. Everything happened as before, but this time the fairy baby was playing with an apple. Kate heard one of the fairies say, "A bite of that apple would make the sick prince as well as ever he was." So Kate rolled all the nuts to the fairy baby until the apple was dropped, and Kate put it in her apron.

As the cockerel crowed they set off again,

but instead of cracking her nuts as she used to, Kate cut up the apple.

"Oh!" said the sick prince, "I wish I could have a bite of that apple."

Kate gave him a bite of the apple, and he rose up quite well, dressed himself, and sat down by the fire, and when the folk came in next morning they found Kate and the young prince cracking nuts and talking happily together.

So Kate and the prince were married in a grand ceremony, as she had wished. Meanwhile, the young prince's brother had fallen in love with Kate's sister, Anne. They too were married and both couples lived happily ever after.

The Princess and the Raven

An extract from **The Wonder Clock**
by Howard Pyle

ONCE UPON A TIME there was a king who had three daughters — the two eldest were handsome, but the youngest, whose name was Golden Hair, was the prettiest maiden to be found within the four ends of the earth.

One day the king went out hunting with all his people. Towards evening he found himself alone and lost in the forest. The

further he went, the less able he was to find the road home again. As the king wandered he came to a tree where a great raven sat. It was as black as chimney soot and had eyes that glowed like two burning coals.

"And where are you going, King?" said the black raven.

"I don't know," said the king, "For I am lost and don't know the way home."

34

"See now," said the raven, "I will show you the way, if you will give me your youngest daughter to be my wife."

"Oh, no," said the king, "I can never do such a thing as that."

"Very well, then," said the raven, "off I go, and here you will have to stay."

Now one will do much before one will stay in a dark forest forever, and so the king promised at last that if the raven would show him the way home, it should have Princess Golden Hair for its wife. The king thought he would easily be able to outwit the bird. So the raven showed him the way out of the forest.

"Tomorrow," it said, "I'll come for my bride, your youngest daughter."

When the next morning came, there was the great black raven sitting outside of the castle gateway waiting for Princess Golden Hair to be sent to him.

But it was not the princess whom he got after all, for the king had told the shepherd to dress his daughter in the princess's dress, and it was she who went to the great black raven instead.

The raven took the shepherd's daughter on its back and away it flew over woods and meadows, until it came to a little hut that stood on a bleak hill. In the hut was a table, and on the table stood a golden goblet of red wine, a silver cup of white wine, and an earthenware jug full of bitter beer.

"This is our home," said the raven, "and now will my dear one drink refreshment after her long and tiresome journey?"

The shepherd's daughter went to the table and took a good drink of the beer. The raven knew that she was no true princess to be happy with bitter beer out of an earthenware jug, when she could have good red wine from a golden goblet. "Come," said the raven, "home we go!" He took her upon his back and flew until they arrived back at the king's castle.

"See," said the raven, "this is not the one I want. Let me have my true bride or you will suffer for it."

The king was frightened. "Very well," said he, "come tomorrow and you shall have your true bride."

When the next morning came, there was the raven waiting. But it was not the princess that he got. The king had ordered the steward's daughter to wear one of the princess's dresses. So the raven took her on his back and flew till he came to the little hut on top of the bleak hill. There stood the golden goblet, the silver cup and the earthenware jug just as before. And now would not the dear maiden drink a drop after her long journey?

Yes, indeed, so she took a good drink of the white wine in the silver cup. But the raven saw that she was no true princess, or she would never have been contented with the silver cup.

"Come," said he, "home we go again, for you are not the bride I seek." So away he flew to the king's castle. "Tomorrow morning," he said to the king, "I will come for the true princess again, and if I do not get her this time you will suffer, for I will tear down your castle about your ears!"

Now the king was terribly frightened. The next morning when the raven came it was

Princess Golden Hair herself whom he got. Up he took her on his back and away he flew with her.

The princess did nothing but weep, so when they came to the little hut, she was glad enough to drink a drop. She didn't look at the earthenware jug or the silver cup, but going straight to the golden goblet she drank the good red wine.

Then all of a sudden the hut grew until it changed into a splendid castle. The black raven changed into the most handsome prince in the world. It was love at first sight!

The prince kissed Princess Golden Hair and said, "I have found my true bride at last. You have freed me and my castle and all of my people from an enchantment. My wicked stepmother laid spells upon us that could only be broken when a real princess

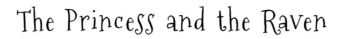

The Princess and the Raven

drank from the golden goblet."
And so they were married, and a
fine wedding they
had of it, I
can tell you!